A Note to Parents and Caregivers:

Read-it! Readers are for children who are just starting on the amazing road to reading. These beautiful books support both the acquisition of reading skills and the love of books.

The RED LEVEL presents familiar topics using common words and repeating sentence patterns.
The BLUE LEVEL presents new ideas using a larger vocabulary and varied sentence structure.
The YELLOW LEVEL presents more challenging ideas, a broad vocabulary, and wide variety in sentence structure.

When sharing a book with your child, read in short stretches, pausing often to talk about the pictures. Have your child turn the pages and point to the pictures and familiar words. And be sure to reread favorite stories or parts of stories.

There is no right or wrong way to share books with children. Find time to read with your child, and pass on the legacy of literacy.

Adria F. Klein, Ph.D.
Professor Emeritus
California State University
San Bernardino, California

First American edition published in 2003 by
Picture Window Books
5115 Excelsior Boulevard
Suite 232
Minneapolis, MN 55416
1-877-845-8392
www.picturewindowbooks.com

First published in Great Britain by Franklin Watts, 96 Leonard Street, London, EC2A 4XD
Text © Barrie Wade 2001
Illustration © Julie Monks 2001

Printed in the United States of America.

Library of Congress Cataloging-in-Publication Data
Wade, Barrie.
  Cinderella / written by Barrie Wade ; illustrated by Julie Monks.—1st American ed.
    p. cm. — (Read-it! fairy tale readers)
  Summary: Although mistreated by her stepmother and stepsisters, Cinderella meets her
prince with the help of her fairy godmother.
  ISBN 1-4048-0052-2
  [1. Fairy tales. 2. Folklore.] I. Monks, Julie, ill. II. Title. III. Series
  PZ8.W117 Ci 2003
  398.2'0944'02—dc21
        [E]   2002072299

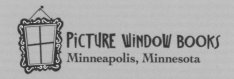

PICTURE WINDOW BOOKS
Minneapolis, Minnesota

Read-it! Readers
Yellow Level

Cinderella

Written by Barry Wade

Illustrated by Julie Monks

Reading Advisors:
Adria F. Klein, Ph.D.
Professor Emeritus, California State University
San Bernardino, California

Ruth Thomas
Durham Public Schools
Durham, North Carolina

R. Ernice Bookout
Durham Public Schools
Durham, North Carolina

Picture Window Books
Minneapolis, Minnesota

Once upon a time there was a beautiful young girl called Cinderella.

Cinderella had two ugly stepsisters who were very cruel to her.

They made Cinderella do
all the hard work.

The two ugly sisters were
invited to the ball
at the royal palace.

Cinderella wished that she could go, too.

Suddenly, a fairy appeared. "I'm your fairy godmother," she told Cinderella.

She waved her magic
wand.

Cinderella's rags turned into a beautiful dress.

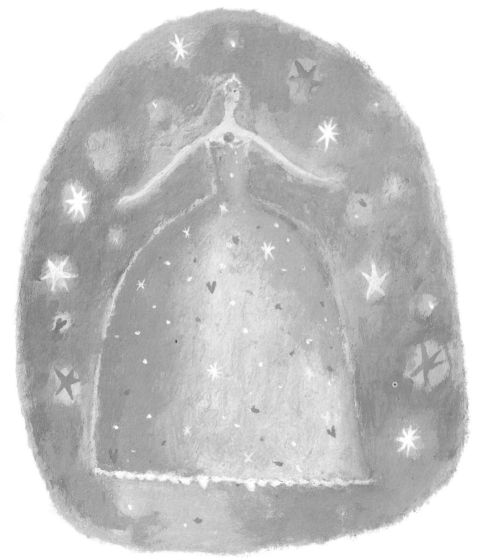

On her feet were sparkling
glass slippers.

The fairy godmother turned a pumpkin into an amazing coach.

Then she turned some
mice into horses.

"Have fun," she said to Cinderella, "but be back by midnight or else!"

"I will!" cried Cinderella.
"Thank you!"

At the ball, everyone wondered who the beautiful princess was.

The prince danced every
dance with her.

When the clock began to strike twelve, Cinderella remembered her promise.

She ran back to the coach.
On the way, she lost one
of her glass slippers.

Suddenly the coach and
horses disappeared.

Cinderella's beautiful dress turned back to rags.

The prince found the glass slipper, but he could not find Cinderella.

Every girl in the kingdom tried on the glass slipper, but it didn't fit.

The ugly sisters tried to fit
into the slipper, but their
feet were much too big.

"Let this girl try it on," said the prince when he saw Cinderella.

"But that's only Cinderella,"
cried the ugly sisters.
"The slipper won't fit her!"

But it did!

So the prince found his
princess, and they lived
happily ever after.

Red Level

The Best Snowman, by Margaret Nash 1-4048-0048-4
Bill's Baggy Pants, by Susan Gates 1-4048-0050-6
Cleo and Leo, by Anne Cassidy 1-4048-0049-2
Felix on the Move, by Maeve Friel 1-4048-0055-7
Jasper and Jess, by Anne Cassidy 1-4048-0061-1
The Lazy Scarecrow, by Jillian Powell 1-4048-0062-X
Little Joe's Big Race, by Andy Blackford 1-4048-0063-8
The Little Star, by Deborah Nash 1-4048-0065-4
The Naughty Puppy, by Jillian Powell 1-4048-0067-0
Selfish Sophie, by Damian Kelleher 1-4048-0069-7

Blue Level

The Bossy Rooster, by Margaret Nash 1-4048-0051-4
Jack's Party, by Ann Bryant 1-4048-0060-3
Little Red Riding Hood, by Maggie Moore 1-4048-0064-6
Recycled!, by Jillian Powell 1-4048-0068-9
The Sassy Monkey, by Anne Cassidy 1-4048-0058-1
The Three Little Pigs, by Maggie Moore 1-4048-0071-9

Yellow Level

Cinderella, by Barrie Wade 1-4048-0052-2
The Crying Princess, by Anne Cassidy 1-4048-0053-0
Eight Enormous Elephants, by Penny Dolan 1-4048-0054-9
Freddie's Fears, by Hilary Robinson 1-4048-0056-5
Goldilocks and the Three Bears, by Barrie Wade 1-4048-0057-3
Mary and the Fairy, by Penny Dolan 1-4048-0066-2
Jack and the Beanstalk, by Maggie Moore 1-4048-0059-X
The Three Billy Goats Gruff, by Barrie Wade 1-4048-0070-0